PUFFIN BOOKS

THE SQUIRREL WIFE

Jack is a poor swine-herd, cruelly treated by his brother; but only he is brave enough that stormy night to answer a distant cry for help. Deep in the forest one of the green people is in trouble.

As a reward for his courage and kindness, Jack is given a magic ring, and the promise of a wife who will show him all the secrets of the forest. The promise is kept, but Jack's adventures are only just beginning.

Philippa Pearce has created an original, richly evocative fairy-story which seems to echo in the imagination with memories of ancient folk-tales and fairy-tales. William Geldart's delicate illustrations are an inspiration.

Philippa Pearce grew up in a mill-house near Cambridge. The house, the river and the village feature in many of her best loved children's books. She was educated at the Perse Girls' School in Cambridge and then at Girton College, Cambridge, where she read English and History. In addition to writing a great many books, she has also worked for the BBC as a scriptwriter-producer, as a children's book editor, as a freelance writer in radio for children and as a book reviewer, lecturer and story-teller. Her now classic books in Puffin include Carnegie Medal winner, *Tom's Midnight Garden*, *What the Neighbours Did and Other Stories*, *A Dog so Small* and *The Battle of Bubble and Squeak*, which won the Whitbread Award. Philippa Pearce lives in Cambridgeshire.

Other books by Philippa Pearce

PHILIPPA PEARCE

Illustrated by William Geldart

PUFFIN BOOKS

PUFFIN BOOKS

Published by the Penguin Group
Penguin Books Ltd, 27 Wrights Lane, London W8 5TZ, England
Penguin Books USA Inc., 375 Hudson Street, New York, New York 10014, USA
Penguin Books Australia Ltd, Ringwood, Victoria, Australia
Penguin Books Canada Ltd, 10 Alcorn Avenue, Toronto, Ontario, Canada M4V 3B2
Penguin Books (NZ) Ltd, 182–190 Wairau Road, Auckland 10, New Zealand

Penguin Books Ltd, Registered Offices: Harmondsworth, Middlesex, England

First published by Longman Young Books, 1971
Published in Puffin Books, 1992
3 5 7 9 10 8 6 4 2

Printed in England by Clays Ltd, St Ives plc
Filmset in Monophoto Baskerville

For my daughter
Sally Christie

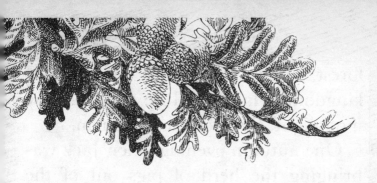

Once upon a time, long ago, on the edge of a great forest, there lived two brothers who were swineherds. The elder brother was very unkind to the younger brother, called Jack. He made him do all the work and gave him hardly enough to eat.

Every day in the autumn Jack drove the pigs into the forest to eat the fallen acorns and the beech-mast and to rootle in the earth. As he set off, his brother always gave him the same warning: 'Don't take the pigs deep into the forest, and be sure to bring them home before sunset, because of the green people.'

The green people were the fairy-people who lived in the heart of the forest; and the forest was their kingdom. They could be seen only by moonlight. Everyone feared them.

One autumn evening when Jack was bringing the herd of pigs out of the forest as usual, he noticed that a wind was beginning to get up. It whirled the leaves from the trees and tossed their branches wildly. By the time the pigs were in their sties and Jack in the cottage which he shared with his brother, a storm was blowing.

That night, when the two brothers had gone to bed, they could not sleep for the howling of the wind round their

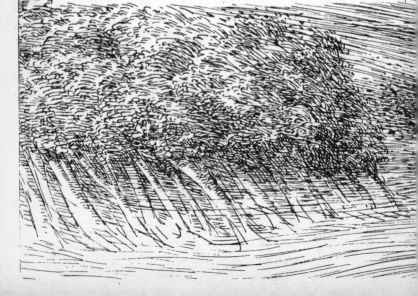

cottage. In the middle of the storm they heard the crash of a great tree falling in the distance, from the direction of the forest.

'Did you hear that?' Jack whispered.

'What a fool you are, Jack!' said his brother. 'Of course I heard the tree falling.'

'But did you hear nothing else?' said Jack. 'There it goes again – listen!'

They both listened and, over the howling of the storm, heard a strange voice far off, crying for help.

'There!' said Jack.

'I heard nothing,' said his brother.

'But you must have heard it: someone calling from the forest.'

'I tell you, I heard nothing. And if there were someone calling, this is not the kind of night to go out helping strangers. Be quiet and go to sleep, or it will be the worse for you.'

So Jack held his tongue.

At last the gale blew itself out and then the elder brother fell asleep, but not Jack. As soon as he heard his brother snoring, he crept out of bed and left the cottage. As he went, he stuck his wood-axe into his belt, as protection against wild beasts or any other enemies.

He took the moonlit way that led to the forest. He reached the very edge of

the forest, hesitated, and then plunged
in. Almost at once he came upon the
great tree – a beech tree – whose
crashing fall he had heard that night.

The tree lay with its trunk full length
upon the ground, its roots torn up into
the air and its leaves smashed down
into the earth. It was all black and
silvery grey in the moonlight; and then

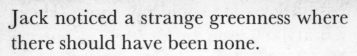

Jack noticed a strange greenness where there should have been none.

He looked closely and saw what at first he thought was a child – a green child; but this was a man, perfectly formed in every way, and yet only the height of a child, and green. He was one of the green people.

The green man had been trapped by the fall of the tree, for it had fallen

across his legs. He could not move. He stared at Jack, and Jack stared at him; but neither said a word. Jack took the wood-axe from his belt and began to hack him free. When he had done this, Jack expected the green man to escape at once back into the depths of the forest. But the green man lay as before, and Jack saw that one of his legs had been crushed by the fall of the tree.

What was to be done? Jack could not bear to carry the green man home to his

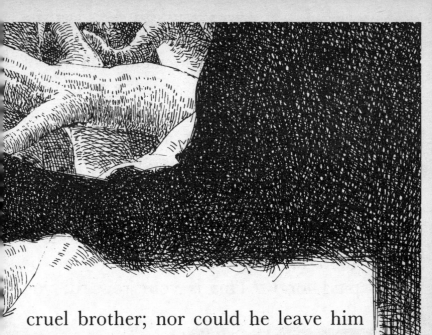

cruel brother; nor could he leave him here, where his own people might never find him. Jack looked at the green man, and the green man looked at Jack, and neither said a word; but Jack knew what he must do. Although he was afraid to do it, he must carry the green man back to his own people in the heart of the forest. He picked him up in his arms – he was as light as a child – and began to carry him deeper and deeper into the forest.

At last, in the heart of the forest, Jack came to a clearing where, by moonlight, he saw a company of the

green people on horseback. Two of them came to him at once and took the injured man from him, all without a word being spoken on either side.

Then one who was clearly lord of them all beckoned to Jack.

Jack knelt and the lord of the green people said, 'Jack, you have done a good night's work and deserve to be paid for it. This is your reward: you

shall enjoy the secrets of our forest through your wife.'

Jack dared respectfully to point out that he had no wife, nor any thought of one as yet.

'I know that,' said the lord of the green people, 'just as I know that you are Jack the swineherd, living on the edge of our forest. Now take this gold ring.' He took a ring from his finger as he spoke, and held it out to Jack. It was a plain gold ring, like a wedding-ring. Jack took it and thanked him for it; but the lord of the green people had not finished with Jack. 'You will wear

this ring upon your finger,' he said, 'until the spring comes.

'In spring the squirrels build their dreys in the trees of our forest and bear their young. At that time you must climb up to a nest where there is a new-born female squirrel and put this ring over its left forepaw, like a bracelet. Then come away.'

'But, sir,' said Jack, 'would not this be a cruel thing to do? For the young squirrel will grow and the ring will stay the same size.'

The lord of the green people laughed. 'Jack, I think you are sometimes a fool, as your brother says. For this is a magic ring, that will grow as the wearer grows; and at the time when squirrels are full grown, you shall find what you shall find.

'And now, Jack, turn and follow your path home, and do not look behind you until you are within sight of it.'

Jack turned as he was told.

He looked down, and there at his feet was a path, white in the moonlight, where he could have sworn there had

never been one before. He followed it, without once looking back, until he came to the very edge of the forest and within sight of the cottage where he lived. Then he looked back and saw that there was no path behind him: it

had vanished behind him as he went forward upon it.

Jack got home and back into bed without his brother's waking, so that his brother never knew what had happened that night. Nor did he seem to notice the gold ring that Jack now wore on his finger – perhaps because it was a fairy ring and invisible to him.

Time passed and time passed, and the time came for squirrels to build their dreys in the forest.

As he had been told, Jack climbed tree after tree.

He searched for a squirrel to which he might give his ring. At last he found

one – a female, new-born, tiny as a rat, hairless and blind as yet. He slipped the gold ring over her left forepaw, so that it rested just above it like a bracelet. Then he climbed down the tree and came away.

Time passed and time passed, and autumn came, when squirrels are full grown. Jack was driving the pigs into the forest as usual to eat acorns and beech-mast and rootle in the earth. As he went by a woodland pool that he had often passed before, he saw someone at the edge of it, kneeling. It

was a girl, who was staring at her reflection in the water as if in amazement. When she heard Jack's footfall stirring the leaves and twigs on the forest floor, she sprang up at once, more like a wild animal than a woman, and stood facing him.

Jack had never seen her before. She was small for a woman, graceful and exceedingly nimble in her movement.

Her hair was brown; her eyes were brown, and what made them remarkable was their strange, wild look of watchfulness.

Jack stared and stared at the strange girl. She smiled at him as though she knew him, and stretched out her left hand towards him. Then he saw that she was wearing a bracelet round the

wrist – a bracelet of plain gold, just like a wedding-ring but, of course, much larger.

'Jack,' said the girl, '– you are Jack, aren't you? – I am your squirrel-wife.'

Then with joy Jack remembered the promise of the lord of the green people. He took the hand she held out towards him, for he knew that already he loved his squirrel-wife, as she loved him. They would live together always, as man and wife. They determined not to go back to Jack's cruel brother, but to settle far from him, within the forest.

The forest was the only place for a squirrel-wife.

And there among the trees they would live happily.

So Jack divided the herd of pigs into two equal parts. One half of the herd he beat back towards his brother's

cottage; the other half he took as his rightful share. Then, driving the pigs before them, Jack and his squirrel-wife went further and further into the forest.

On and on through the forest they went, until at last they came almost

out at the other side – the side of the forest furthest from where Jack had lived with his brother. Here Jack built them a cottage and pig-sties and here they settled.

They lived very happily, and they prospered. Jack tended the pigs as before; but now he began also to make tables and chairs and many other things from the different woods of the forest.

His squirrel-wife knew all the trees of the forest: oak, ash, beech, birch and the rest. She could tell him exactly which wood was best for each purpose.

She would set her ear to the tree-trunks, and could tell which tree was sound all through and which was rotten, wholly or in the smallest degree. She could lay her hand upon a tree and tell its age exactly, even before Jack had cut it down and counted its year-rings. She knew where the best blackberries were to be found, and the best mushrooms. She knew where the wild bees stored their honey and – of course – where the squirrels stored their nuts. It was just as the lord of the green people had promised: Jack could enjoy the secrets of the forest through his squirrel-wife.

Jack and his squirrel-wife spent all their time in the forest, except when they took a pigling or a table or a chair to sell in the village just outside. The villagers bought Jack's wares, but at the same time, they distrusted him, because of his wife. They were afraid of the squirrel-wife on account of that strange, watchful look in her eyes. The forest-woman, they called her.

Word of Jack and his forest-woman was passed from that village to the next, and so from village to village, until at last it reached Jack's elder brother, far away on the other side of the forest. He was so enraged to hear of Jack's happiness that he travelled all round the edge of the forest – a journey of many days – until he reached the village where Jack was best known.

There, he spread the story that Jack was a runaway thief.

'He sells you piglings that are by rights my piglings,' he said to the villagers. 'For this slippery brother of mine disappeared into the forest one day, taking with him half my herd of pigs. He is a thief, and I demand his punishment.'

The villagers listened and nodded and said that Jack had seemed an honest man, but then indeed how could any honest man have such a wife as Jack had? So they were willing to

believe the falsehoods told them by
Jack's brother; and when Jack next
came to the village they seized him and
threw him into prison.

Their prison was a room with a
barred window and a locked door at
the top of a tower. The key of the door
was given into the charge of Jack's own
brother. He had a room at the bottom
of the tower to sleep in. Here he hung
the key of Jack's prison from a nail on
the wall.

Poor Jack looked out from his prison
window towards the forest; he could
see it, but he feared he might never go
there freely again. He looked
downwards from his window and could
see his squirrel-wife, for she stood at
the foot of the tower, weeping. The end

of the day had come, and the squirrel-wife now turned away from the tower towards the forest, still weeping. Jack called to her to come back; but she would not. 'I must go into the forest,' she said, 'to find the green people.'

'Oh, take care!' cried Jack. 'What do you mean to ask them?'

'Nothing. I mean only to give back to them my gold bracelet.'

'But then you would be a squirrel again!'

'That is what I want; that is what I need to be, if I am to help you.'

'Don't go!' cried Jack, shaking the bars of his window in frenzy. 'Don't go! Don't go!'

But the squirrel-wife had already gone, leaving Jack in despair.

The sun set. Darkness came, and then moonlight – full moonlight; and Jack was still looking out from his prison window. Everything was quiet except for the sound of Jack's brother

snoring in bed in the room below. Then Jack heard a scrabbling sound in the ivy that grew on the prison-tower. He looked down and saw, by moonshine, a

squirrel that was slipping through his brother's open window. The sound of snoring never stopped, but in a moment the squirrel was out again with something glinting between its teeth – a key. Now it was climbing up the ivy – up – up to Jack's window. It slipped in between the bars of the window and dropped the key into the palm of his outstretched hand. Then it leapt upon his shoulder and laid its head against his cheek.

Using this key, Jack unlocked his prison-door and – with the squirrel still on his shoulder – crept out and down the stairway. He could hear his brother's steady snoring as he stole past the door where he slept. He reached the heavy outside door that would let him go free from the tower altogether. He tried it, afraid that he would find it locked; but it was not. He began to ease it open. Its hinges were rusty and

stiff and, as the door opened bit by bit, they creaked. At the loudest creak, the snoring stopped. 'What is it?' called the sleepy voice of Jack's brother. 'Who goes there?' Then fully awake, he shouted: 'The prisoner is escaping! Stop thief! Stop!'

By now Jack was already clear of the tower and running as fast as he could towards the forest, with the squirrel clinging to his shoulder. After him came his brother; and after his brother came the villagers, roused from their beds and taking up the cry: 'Stop thief!'

Jack reached the trees and at once plunged among them, and his brother and all the villagers, forgetting their fear of the forest by moonlight, plunged after him. But, as Jack and his squirrel fled before them deeper and deeper into the forest, the shouting behind them

grew fainter. Soon they could hear it no longer.

They went on until at last they came to a moonlit clearing, where a company of the green people was assembled. With his squirrel on his shoulder, Jack went forward.

He knelt humbly before the lord of the green people. The lord was frowning: 'You have noisy friends, Jack, who follow you into our forest.'

'No friends of mine, sir,' said Jack, 'but I ask your pardon all the same.'

'Is that all you have come to ask us?'

'No, sir,' said Jack, but did not dare yet to say more.

The lord of the green people said: 'First you came to us and were rewarded handsomely with the gift of a golden ring, that grew in size to a bracelet. Then – this very night – your squirrel-wife came to return that gift to

the givers. And now you come back
together – Jack and his squirrel who
was once a squirrel-wife – to ask
something more of us.

'Before you ask, Jack, remember this.
Fairy gifts cannot be given twice.'

'I do not ask for the ring or for the
bracelet again,' Jack said, 'but I want
my squirrel-wife.'

The lord of the green people shook
his head. 'No, Jack. We cannot give

you your squirrel-wife a second time. But this we will do for you: you can have either the squirrel on your shoulder or your wife by your side. Which? You must decide.'

Jack was bewildered by these words, and hesitated. Then he said, 'Sir, a man wants a wife by his side. I choose my wife.'

For the first time the lord of the green people smiled. 'I think you are not always the fool your brother calls

you, Jack. You have chosen wisely. You shall have your wife, and you need fear no harm either from your brother or from the people of the village.

'We shall keep your brother safe with us in the forest until he learns a little wisdom; and we shall send the rest home to their beds. We shall wipe from their minds all memory of the evil they once believed of you both. And now, Jack, turn and follow your path home. You shall find what you shall find.'

As once before, Jack turned and followed a fairy path, white in the moonlight. The squirrel was still on his

shoulder and, as he went, he grew amazed at its heaviness.

At last he had to stop to rest. Then he looked over his shoulder, and lo and behold! he was carrying not a squirrel at all, but a young woman – his wife.

She slipped down to the ground beside him and he hugged her in his arms. She seemed to be his squirrel-wife, exactly as he had always known her; but now she pressed close to him

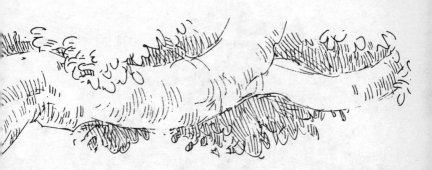

for protection, shivering as if in dread.

She said, 'Dear Jack, I fear the forest – I don't know how I could ever have wished to live here. I have one thing to beg of you. When we get home, let us gather the herd of pigs and all your tools and our household goods, and let us take them out of the forest and settle in the village. We must live like other people, because now I am like other women.'

Looking into her eyes, Jack could no

longer see that strange watchfulness
that had made her seem like a wild
creature. It had vanished altogether.
Then he knew that she was no longer
partly squirrel and partly woman – a
squirrel-wife; she was all woman now,
according to the choice he had made
before the lord of the green people.

'Dear wife,' said Jack, 'we shall do
just as you wish.'

So they moved all their belongings

and settled in the village just outside the forest. The villagers welcomed them, for they had lost all memory of Jack and his wife as they had once been. Jack herded pigs and made tables and chairs as before; his wife cooked and cleaned and minded the babies that were born, but she had lost her knowledge of the secrets of the forest.

Nor did she wish to go into the forest again: for she said that the tall trees made her afraid, even by daylight.

By moonlight, nobody would go into the forest, because of the green people.

So Jack and his wife lived happily on the edge of the forest and had children and grandchildren and great-grandchildren.

As for Jack's elder brother, the green people kept him as their servant for a thousand years, until he had learned a little wisdom.

Some other Young Puffin Story Books

THE ELM STREET LOT
Philippa Pearce

Mr Crackenthorpe was a surly old fellow, but he might have been forgiven for his suspicions. For the Elm Street gang were always in on the action, whether they were tracking down a lost hamster, being galley-slaves in a brand-new bathtub, or going on safari across the roof-tops!

LION AT SCHOOL AND OTHER STORIES
Philippa Pearce

A growling lion spends a morning at school and frightens the school bully; a little boy saves a mouse's life; and the magic Great Sharp Scissors cause havoc! These are just some of the surprises in store in this charming collection of nine lively tales.

THE SLIPPERS THAT TALKED
Gyles Brandreth

Michelle thinks that her seventh birthday is going to be the best ever. But it isn't – it is the worst. For a start, it's Sunday and her parents wake up late. There is no post and her presents are boring. Then Michelle is sick – and that's when the fun starts!

What look like a boring old pair of slippers turn out to be the most exciting birthday present Michelle has ever had!

A perfect read for anyone who has ever had a birthday.

ALLOTMENT LANE IN LONDON
Margaret Joy

No one in Miss Mee's class has ever been to London before, so everybody is really excited about this term's school trip. With a boat trip on the river, visits to a market, museums and the zoo, and even an unexpected lesson in rhyming slang, there's a lot to fit in to four days. So keep together everyone, and don't get lost! The children from Allotment Lane School have great fun (and a few frights) in this entertaining collection of stories.

HENRY AND THE SEA
Joe Buffalo Stuart and Alexander Stuart

When Henry goes to live by the sea, he's more interested in the video games on the pier than anything else. Until one day the Sea not only talks to him but magics itself into an empty paper cup. An exciting and hilarious friendship begins which takes Henry and the Sea to some rather unusual places – and leaves the rest of the world wondering where the waves went!

JEFFREY'S JOKE MACHINE
Alexander McCall Smith

Everyone likes a good laugh, and Jeffrey can't believe his luck when he finds an old joke machine which really works. Soon people are queuing up for their very own joke, and laughing till they cry. But then something goes badly wrong – has the joke machine lost its sense of humour? Or could it have something to do with bad-tempered Mr Jenkinson, who lost his years ago?

THE RED SECRET
Jenny Nimmo

When the Turner family leaves London to live in a small village in Shropshire, Tom and his sister Daisy feel very left out. The village children are suspicious of them and are reluctant to make friends. However, when he is given a strange present by a boy in his class, Tom is drawn into an adventure which results in acceptance and new friends for both himself and Daisy.

BONESHAKER
Paul and Emma Rogers

She's old, a bit dusty and a bit rusty, but Oliver knows she's a very special bicycle. For Boneshaker has a mind of her own. With a bike like her, life's bound to be exciting, and these four stories are full of races, rescues and breathtaking rides!

THE INTERGALACTIC KITCHEN
Frank Rodgers

When the red light on Mr Bird's safety and protection system signals a class 1A emergency, Mrs Bird and her children follow the instructions. To their amazement they blast off into space in their kitchen.

The family's adventures in their intergalactic kitchen are told using a wonderful mix of text and comic strip, making this story fantastic fun to read.

THE SPY BEFORE YESTERDAY
Catherine Storr

'My dad was a spy . . .' Ben is surrounded by interesting and un-usual friends with extraordinary names or extraordinary relations, or they're extraordinarily clever at something. But Ben is just Ben, and his dad is ordinary Old Harris, the Head and maths teacher. But has his dad never been anything more? Ben's imagination de-velops until even he begins to wonder where the truth really lies.

KING KEITH AND THE NASTY CASE
OF DRAGONITUS
Kaye Umansky

When cowardly King Keith goes down with a right royal cold, he refuses to take his horrid medicine. So how can he possibly persuade a tearful, spotty dragon with the dreaded Dragonitus to be brave and take *his* nasty medicine?

King Keith is in a right royal sulk. His show-off cousin King Clive has invited himself to tea. They never liked each other before – will they be able to settle old scores?

Two lively and entertaining right royal stories for young readers to enjoy.

MYSTERY AT MUSKET BAY
Tony Bradman

Trelawney the parrot is certain Dead Man Island is haunted. He won't stop squawking about it! But the rest of the Bluebeard family think there might be more to the mystery of Musket Bay when they find strange footprints in the sand. Would a real ghost leave foot-prints? Follow the mysterious trail with them and join in the fun.

This is the third story about the Bluebeards pirate family and their adventures.

THE RAILWAY CAT AND THE HORSE
Phyllis Arkle

Alfie and his friends are very curious to learn that a valuable horse is going to be delivered to their station. Could it be a racehorse, they wonder? They soon find out that it's no ordinary horse, but one that's going to need very special treatment.

THE HODGEHEG
Dick King-Smith

The story of Max, the hedgehog who becomes a hodgeheg, who becomes a hero. The hedgehog family of Number 5A are a happy bunch but they dream of reaching the Park across the road. Unfortunately, a very busy road lies between them and their goal and no one has found a way to cross it in safety. No one, that is, until the determined young Max decides to solve the problem once and for all . . .

STICK TO IT, CHARLIE
Joy Allen

In these two 'Charlie' adventures, Charlie meets a new friend and finds a new interest – playing the piano. The new friend proves his worth when Charlie and the gang find themselves in a tight spot. As for the piano – well, even football comes second place!